The
Greatest
Christmas
Gift

The Greatest Christmas Gift

TIAH RODRIGUEZ-CRAWL

TATE PUBLISHING
AND **ENTERPRISES,** LLC

Published by Tate Publishing & Enterprises, LLC
127 E. Trade Center Terrace | Mustang, Oklahoma 73064 USA
1.888.361.9473 | www.tatepublishing.com

Tate Publishing is committed to excellence in the publishing industry. The company reflects the philosophy established by the founders, based on Psalm 68:11,
"The Lord gave the word and great was the company of those who published it."

Book design copyright © 2014 by Tate Publishing, LLC. All rights reserved.
Cover design by Rodrigo Adolfo
Interior design by Manolito Bastasa

Published in the United States of America

ISBN: 978-1-63268-640-4
Fiction / General
14.07.31

This book is dedicated to my son, James. My greatest joy in life has been, and always will be, being your mother. Some of my fondest memories of your childhood include the times I told you stories to pass the time during our long commutes. How your eyes would light up and your imagination accept the invitation to experience every story as if they were real and you were actually there! Thank you for always being my inspiration.

CONTENTS

THE PHONE CALL

The long-awaited phone call came at 8:00 p.m. James was excited to hear his mom's voice. He expected her to be calling from the local airport to say she had arrived. Instead, his anxious smile quickly faded as he learned his mother's flight had never left New York City.

"I'm sorry, my love!" his mother reported over the phone. "The weather has been so severe the airports have shut down. Maybe I can see you in a few days when the weather calms down."

James sighed with disappointment. He struggled to speak, his eyes flooding with tears. "But, Mom, tomorrow's Christmas, and I haven't seen you in a month. I miss you, Mom." His words seemed to choke him as he fought the desire to cry out loud. James swallowed his emotions with a huge gulp, but the lump continued to grab him by the throat.

His mother could feel his disappointment through the phone. "Baby, I know the separation has been rough on you, but I need you to know that I love and miss you, too!

Besides, I have a surprise for you, and I'm just as anxious as you are for me to arrive in Georgia. I'll do my best to make it as soon as I can. I promise. Until then, remember what Christmas is really about—love. And I really love you very much! Good-bye, my precious love. I'll see you soon."

James said his reluctant good-bye to his mother and hung up the phone. He understood, but he was still hurting. So many emotions were welling up inside of him. Since his parents' separation almost a year ago, he hadn't been able to see his mother very often. She lived too far away to visit regularly. Even though the divorce had not been finalized yet, James's parents agreed that it would be best for him to live with his father.

The very thought of his parents divorcing was unsettling to him. He knew other kids and families that experienced divorce. So naturally, he worried about the changes the divorce would bring and how they would affect the life he knew. Would his parents fight more now that they had to share custody? How would he decide between being with one parent over the other when all he really wanted was to be with them both? How would he feel if they decided to date? *Unthinkable!* That would mean adding someone else to the family equation. He couldn't even stomach the thought. The whole divorce thing made him sick! Weren't parents supposed to be together forever and love each other 'til death do them part? Maybe that's how it was in the old Shakespeare days.

James went to the window for a view of the park across the street. He saw a couple holding hands as they walked through the park. They seemed to be so happy and in love. As he watched them snuggle together on a park bench, he struggled to comprehend how two people could love each other so very much and then act as if they forgot that they ever did. There were so many unanswered questions.

Why couldn't they love each other the same or even better than before? What's so hard about that, that so many adults choose to quit? Didn't they realize that divorce hurts everyone, that they aren't in it alone? What about the kids, the dog, the grandparents, and the rest of the family? Aren't they important enough to be a part of the decision? James wondered.

What made thinking about his parent's separation and imminent divorce even worse was that it was Christmas Eve. The first Christmas the family would be spending apart.

Why did his dad have to move them away, anyway? Couldn't his dad have found the same job back home? It just didn't seem fair! While he silently compiled all of his complaints on an imaginary list, he couldn't help but notice how small this year's Christmas tree looked. It seemed to be waiting impatiently for some much needed attention. It helplessly leaned to the left in front of the living room window. He smiled as he imagined it almost tipping over in defeat and his mom saving it just in time.

Like his Nana, Jean, Mom was a master decorator and manager of the Christmas spirit every year. She knew how to create such a serene and loving environment at Christmas time, complete with colorful lights, stories, and songs by the tree. She could make the house look like a Christmas card that had come to life! He remembered the winters when he was much younger. Winter walks with Mom always seemed magical. His mother could even make the snow glisten at night. He never really did figure out how she did it.

Suddenly, James could feel his countenance glow with warmth as he smiled and remembered those times. It was almost as if the seemingly depressed and unclothed tree spoke to him. The bare tree seemed to scold him and remind him that there were no presents beneath it. No sooner than the smile appeared on his face, it was wiped away. There weren't any presents under the tree. Not a single one. Mom usually did all of the Christmas shopping. Dad could do it, but Mom was better at it and actually enjoyed shopping at Christmas time. With no presents under the tree, it was clear to James that his mother must have had all the gifts with her at the airport. Now she wasn't even going to make it here for Christmas. As he thought about the presents he wouldn't receive for several weeks, James became increasingly discouraged. "Who celebrates Christmas without any gifts? Everyone will be opening their gifts on Christmas day and I won't have any. This is going to be the worst Christmas ever!" James shouted.

His father was sitting in his favorite chair watching the football game, or trying to at least. James's continuous murmurings, whining, and complaining undoubtedly disturbed his father until he just couldn't take it anymore.

"James, that's enough!" he commanded. "You're forgetting what Christmas is all about. Christmas is about Jesus and His birth! Jesus' birth was a gift of love from God and serves as a reminder from God that we must all give love unselfishly! So instead of thinking about what you don't have and won't get, I want you to spend the rest of the night thinking about how and what you can give to someone else this Christmas!"

James rolled his eyes and blew his breath while his father lectured. Despite his behavior, he was actually listening.

"So, it's not about getting gifts, son. In the meantime, let's be thankful that your mother is safe and you'll get to see her soon, very soon," Dad said patiently. "Now, let's get some pizza…unless, of course, you don't like pizza anymore… Then you can have some brussels sprouts for dinner, instead," he said playfully as he attempted to tickle and wrestle with his son.

James laughed as he counterattacked. "Dad! Cut it out! No fair. You caught me off guard!" he protested. He tried to avoid laughing out loud.

His dad gave him a big wrestling-type hug and pulled James's hat over his eyes as they put on their coats. They continued to laugh and play, which was not unusual for the two. They had a great relationship. James could talk with his dad about anything, and he considered his father to be his hero.

James Sr. always made it a point to teach his son everything he knew and to use everyday life as his lesson plan. James may have never even realized how much of a teacher his father really was, since everyday with Dad was often filled with fun times.

Soon afterward, they left the apartment and walked toward the car. James was reminded of his father's wise words. These were moments he loved—spending time with his dad laughing, joking, and playing. It was memorable events like these that he was truly thankful for.

As the wisdom of his father's words impressed upon his heart, he thought about the moments he loved spending with his mother as well. A thick, growing lump began to form in his throat again, and whether or not the lump was responsible, his eyes sneakily began to flood with tears. It was difficult for him to hold back the tears this time, but he quietly struggled to do so. As he swallowed the lump, the tears finally did retreat just in time to go unnoticed by his dad. At least, that was what he thought.

A VERY WHITE CHRISTMAS

The roads glistened with what appeared to be a thick coating of glazed white snow. It was the first snowfall in the past five years in Marietta. Even more historical was the fact that it was the first time in ten years that Georgia had snowfall on Christmas Eve. James loved the snow. It reminded him of Christmas in Buffalo and New York City—of course, without the usual state of panic that occurred when you put Georgia residents and snow together. Here the schools, stores, and roads would close due to the snow or icy rains, but in New York City or Buffalo life went on. Although James missed New York for a multitude of reasons, he didn't mind school being closed one bit! The weather was pretty intense for driving in Georgia, so James's father drove cautiously.

James was impatient for pizza, as usual, so he asked his father rather simply, "Hey, Dad, why didn't we have the pizza delivered?"

"Are you kidding?" his father replied. "They won't drive out here in this weather! The snow is only four inches deep, and they're already prepared to declare a state of emergency." They both laughed hard and loud at the thought of such a scene.

"Oh, yeah. You're right," James agreed.

"Well, to tell you the truth, even if they were willing to deliver tonight, we would probably be waiting too long for it to get here. We'd be waiting so long, our dog, Jada, would start looking like a steak dinner!" his father teased.

"Dad!" James said, laughing at his father's silliness.

James Sr. continued making silly jokes about anything and everything. They laughed and laughed! James suddenly realized he was no longer feeling sad. His father always seemed to know how to make him feel better whenever he was down. He loved that about his dad. He continued listening and watching as his father laughed at his own simple jokes. James smiled inside at the sight of seeing his father happy.

Just a few more blocks and they would be at the pizzeria. It wasn't New York style pizza, but James knew it would be good. As his father became increasingly focused on the ice-laden streets, James observed the shy silence of the town. Most of the businesses were closed. The bad weather rendered the streets bare and almost deserted. Without the bright and lively animation of the storefront Christmas lights and decorations, it really was becoming a silent night after all. *I guess some cities do sleep*, James thought.

No Christmas Eve is ever really complete without snow. At least that's how James felt, but what really made Christmas Eve enchanting was the Christmas music he was accustomed to hearing around the holidays. As they drove, James cut the car radio on and raised the volume. He heard some of his favorites like "Sleigh Ride" and "Have a Holly, Jolly Christmas" interrupted by the windshield wipers as they danced back and forth across the windshield.

The ride to the pizzeria was slow, but it gave James the opportunity to truly listen and observe his community. As they got closer to the shopping plaza, the streets seemed to come alive again. He noticed a few pedestrians hurrying into stores to make last-minute purchases. He admired the Christmas decorations draped like streamers throughout the shops on the main streets as they appeared to be welcoming the holiday season. James especially enjoyed the Christmas lights—some blinking, twinkling, fading and chasing. He likened them to tiny little lamps that had just enough light to make an evening room feel cozy, safe, and warm.

James's mother loved Christmas decorations—the lights especially! He remembered how his mother loved to decorate their home for the holidays. In the evening they'd sit in the living room with all the house lights off and drink hot chocolate while listening to Christmas songs under the huge lit Christmas tree. Sometimes they'd sit on the porch snuggling under a blanket as the cool winter's night blew steam off their mugs of hot chocolate. His mom would tell him stories while they adored the view of snow-covered houses and trees twinkling against the moonlit sky.

James closed his eyes briefly as he imagined being back there, right alongside his mom with her singing Christmas carols with him. He could almost feel the clean, brisk air on his face, and he remembered how the snow-swept New York streets seemed clean and calm late at night. The snow would lay there undisturbed, not a footprint in sight, and the silence of the city was loud, proving, as his mother would say, that "The city did sleep!"

With his eyes still closed, James rolled down his window to get a sniff of the cold winter air, comparing it to the winter air of New York. He missed home so much. Then James sighed a big sigh and opened his eyes. Georgia didn't feel like home yet, at least not without his mom.

The radio played even louder than before, or so it seemed. One of his mom's favorite Christmas songs was playing. It was "Christmas Shoes." His mom would always get teary-eyed every time she heard it. James remembered teasing her about how emotional she got over movies and songs. He didn't understand then why she would get that way. And now, James found himself in her shoes. He smiled at the irony of it all and silently told himself, *Don't cry. Don't cry!* Undetected by his father, the tears did retreat upon his command.

"Finally!" James exclaimed as they turned the corner to the pizzeria.

The pizzeria was slightly crowded with people who obviously thought like his dad did. It was evident that they would have to wait anyway. But James was just glad he was going to get pizza, so a few more minutes wouldn't matter to him. His father briefly reviewed the menu and decided to order one large cheese pizza and two meat lovers pizzas with *extra* pepperoni. He looked at his son for approval. James's eyes glared, his mouth hung open, and his head bobbled up and down excitedly. And with that confirming gesture, the deal was sealed.

"James, we may have to eat pizza for a couple of days," his father stated.

"Fine by me!" James proclaimed.

As his father waited in line to place the order, James chose a booth for them to sit in and wait. He chose a window seat facing Delk Road that gave him a full view of the plaza. James was excited to see that the snow had started up again. He marveled at the uniquely shaped flurries that floated and danced slowly in mid-air as soft winds directed their flight. Looking beyond the flurries, James noticed a family having car trouble down the street. Unable to repair the car, the driver gathered his family and they walked to the bus stop that was directly across from the pizzeria.

James watched as the family huddled together to try to stay warm. He noticed that the family of three was not properly dressed for the weather they were in. The father had on a jacket, but it was too light for the shuffling wind that whistled against the pizzeria windows. The boy was about a year or two younger than James so he must have been six or seven years old. He had no jacket at all, only a long sleeved sweatshirt and a blanket he struggled to wrap himself in. His mother was wearing some sort of woven, blanket-shirt that you put over your head to wear like a sleeveless sweater. It was pink and apple green with orange tassels on the ends. It was like the one his great-grandmother would knit for the women in his family. His mom had one that she wore often, but he couldn't remember what it was called.

James couldn't help but notice that the woman kept fidgeting underneath her blanket-shirt, and at first, he couldn't figure out why. She kept pacing back and forth, rocking her arms up and down, then back and forth. She appeared uncomfortably anxious.

"She really must be cold," James thought out loud.

However, he soon discovered the source of the woman's discontent: she had a baby in her arms! Now James was beginning to feel uncomfortable, almost as if he were the one outside in the cold. As James continued to observe, he realized that they were in for a terrible surprise. The buses were no longer running at this time of night. Especially in this weather. *What will happen to them now?*

The family huddled together, and the father tried to wrap his arms around the bunch as they stood in a corner of the partially enclosed bus stop. James turned to check his father's progress in the line. He hadn't made it very far. It looked like it would be awhile before they were going to get back home. Looking back out the window, James knew it would be the same for the stranded family waiting at the bus stop.

James's imagination brought him back in time to when he was an infant. His mother had told him stories about her daily commute to and from his daycare, college classes, and work in the wintry, snowy city of Buffalo. He envisioned his mother boarding a public bus with her book bag, baby bag, a bundled up baby and his folded stroller. How she managed to do that he didn't know, but it caused him to think on how much parents do with and for their kids.

About five minutes passed, and as he suspected, there still was no bus. No taxis or cars were on the street. The fact that there were no telephone booths available didn't help this family, either. Apparently, the family was now stranded!

The sky thickened with snow. The street lamps were quickly being covered by the freshly blown snow that was transported by the ten-mile-per-hour winds. Despite their struggle to shine brightly, the streets began to dim. The trees no longer danced along the storefronts or in the shopping center's courtyard. They stood tall and lifeless as their frozen limbs seemed to bear the burden of the storm.

The winds grew stronger at times and toppled over garbage cans, sending trash scurrying through the streets. James could hear the wind whistle its wintry tune as it blew across the window and along its hurried path. As the weather worsened, it seemingly taunted the family's determination to survive the storm. They looked desperate and uncertain of what to do.

James anxiously called out, "Hey, Dad! Come here, quick!"

James's father came over with the pizza boxes in hand. "Are you ready to go, Jr.?"

"No, Dad. Well, yeah, but that's not why I called you. Look! See that family over there at the bus stop?" James pointed through the snow-sprayed window. "They have been out there for a while, Dad, and they're freezing! I think their car broke down. It's too cold out there for them, Dad. See the lady rocking back and forth and pacing? All she has on is that pullover blanket thing, like the one Mom has. And see their son? Their son doesn't have on a coat, just a sweatshirt! His dad got a blanket from out of their car and put it around him. The dad must not have anything else to wear either but that light jacket. They must be very cold."

"Aw, man! That's definitely not good. Maybe they called someone. I'm sure they'll be okay. They're just waiting to be picked up," his father said, reassuringly.

"No, Dad. They have been out there for a long time! Actually, for as long as we've been in here. I think they are waiting for the bus, Dad. They don't even know the buses have stopped for the night," he said anxiously. "What will happen to them, Dad?" James inquired.

"I don't know, Jimmy. I'm sure they called someone. But it is really cold out there. We can see if they need to use our phone before we get in the car, okay?" his father suggested.

"Yeah. I haven't seen them use a cell phone out there. What if there isn't anyone they *can* call, Dad? They can't stay out here, even for a little while longer! Hey, Dad," James hesitated but had to ask, "we live nearby and we have lots of pizza. Can we bring them to our house?" James asked pleadingly.

"James, I don't know if they'll even want to do that. They don't know us, James. People aren't typically willing to go with strangers."

Although his father rejected his suggestion, James didn't give up and continued to negotiate. Living up to his mother's nickname as the Great Negotiator.

"But Dad, can't we just ask them? There is no way they'll be safe out here, and I'm sure they'll want to get warm, especially with the baby…"

"A baby? Is that what she's rocking? I thought she was just cold. You know your mother gets cold like that, too. Well, okay. We can ask them. I think that is a great idea, son!"

James smiled and eagerly accompanied his father to invite their Christmas Eve guests over for pizza and some heat! James and his father immediately approached the family to offer their assistance.

"We saw you had some car trouble. Are you waiting for a ride home?" James's father asked.

The husband and his wife did not speak fluent English. James realized now why his mother felt it was so important for him to learn Spanish, especially since he was African American and Puerto Rican. While he could understand parts of what they were saying, he knew he could not effectively communicate with them. Luckily, the couple's son began to translate and replied on behalf of his father.

"No. We were waiting for the bus, but it hasn't come yet. Do you know when we can get the next one?" the young boy said, shivering.

"I'm sorry, but the buses don't run after 8:00 p.m. Would you like to call a cab and then maybe you can come back for the car tomorrow?" suggested James Sr.

After relaying the information to his parents, the young boy's father had a brief discussion with his family.

The boy regretfully replied, "My father thanks you for telling us about the buses. We live too far to take a cab, and it would be too much money. Papa will need that money to repair the car tomorrow. We were going to ride the bus to the underground train station and wait there, where it's warm, until tomorrow morning. Is the train station near here, sir?" the boy asked with teeth chattering.

James's father was chilled to the bone and knew the family had to be hungry and tired. He wasn't sure what their response would be, but he hoped they would accept his invitation. "Listen, it's too cold out here and in the train station. We live close by, and we have plenty of pizza. Ask your family if they would like to be our houseguests tonight. I will be happy to drive you to your home once the storm dies down in the morning. Please, you are welcome to spend Christmas Eve with us."

The family discussed the offer, and with a brief hesitation, finally agreed to be the guests of two unusually hospitable strangers.

Mi Casa es Su Casa

The ride home seemed shorter than the ride to the pizzeria. When the car stopped in front of their home, James rushed out of the passenger seat to open the door for the woman and her baby. His mom taught him to always open the door for ladies and to be a gentleman. She would be proud of him if she could see him now. She'd know that he had been minding her words after all. The woman smiled and thanked him as he led her to the porch. The boy followed behind them, excitedly dragging his father by the hand.

Once inside, James Sr. formally welcomed them into his home. James showed them the extra guest room and gathered their things. He got them towels and washcloths, socks and slippers. It was obvious that they were still cold because it took at least five minutes for them to stop shivering.

While his father got a warm and cozy fire started in the fireplace, James found two of his baby blankets stored away in a box of old stuff that his mother insisted he keep. He pulled them out and gave them to the visiting mother and her baby. She took the blankets and smiled at James, her eyes swelling with gratitude and loving tears.

Her husband admired James's spirit and immediately said, "Thank you so very much!"

James Sr. turned on the television and gave the father the remote. "You can put it on whatever channel you like," he said. "Please, make yourself at home. I'm going to make some hot chocolate for all of you to get warmed up."

James set out the plates, cups, napkins, and pizza. The boy came over to help him set the table. James asked the boy what was his name, and he told him it was Eduardo.

"Really? That's my middle name. See, my dad is African American, and my mom is Puerto Rican and African American. She named me after my father, but wanted my middle name to reflect my Hispanic heritage. Now Mom and I are working on speaking fluent Spanish. It wasn't spoken in her home when she was a little girl, so she feels it's really important we learn how. I guess it's almost the opposite for you and your family, huh?" asked James.

"Yeah. I guess so. My parents are learning more and more English everyday. They take classes at my school through PTA. I practice with them at home every night. My parents think it's very important, too, like your mom."

They talked a little more about their schools, their favorite subjects, and even their favorite lunches. Already they discovered they had so very much in common. When they were done, everyone gathered around the table and simultaneously held hands with one another (as if speaking in a universal language) and prepared to bless the food.

Eduardo's father began speaking, "Please, I would like to pray for you and over the food. Is this okay?" James and his dad nodded and encouraged him to do so. He began with introductions.

"My name is Jose Rodriguez. This is my family: my wife, Manuela; my son, Eduardo; and my daughter, Maria Elisabeth. We thank you for letting us come here in your home. You are very nice to my family. I thank you. Dios bendiga."

James paid close attention to Mr. Rodriguez as he spoke. His voice was strong, clear, and confident. And although his Puerto Rican accent was just as thick as James's great-grandmother's, James understood every word he spoke and admired him for the courage and determination it must take to actually learn another language. Once again, he could see why his mom stressed the importance of taking as much Spanish in school as possible.

Assuming his father had no prior knowledge of Spanish vocabulary, and having finished taking a Spanish test right before Christmas break, James decided to help his father understand. He turned and whispered, "Dad, that means, "God bless you." His father smiled, then nodded affirmatively as Jose began to pray.

Eduardo translated the prayer: "Heavenly Father, we thank you for your goodness and mercy tonight. Bless the food that has been prepared and provided for us. You are always so good. Thank you for James and his son, your children that you have sent to protect and care for us. Bless them, Father, for their kindness and the love they have shown to us tonight. And most of all, thank you for your son who was born this night, our Savior, our shepherd, Jesus the Christ! Amen."

"Amen," the room echoed.

Pizza has a way of bringing people together, James thought. Or was it really the pizza? He wasn't sure and really didn't care to ponder on it. He was too busy having a great time talking, singing, playing video games and eating. Eduardo and his family were enjoying themselves and were becoming more and more comfortable. They admired the Christmas tree that James and his father decorated. They even sang along on one of James's (and his mother's) favorite Christmas songs, "Feliz Navidad!" It was so much fun that James couldn't help but think that his mother was missing a great time.

"Mom would love this, Dad," he uttered with a smile.

"Yes, she would. Your mother loves to entertain and have fun. That's what makes her so wonderful," his Dad remarked.

James's head spun around to look back at his father. He was amazed by his father's comment. It was a long time since he heard his dad say something about his mom, especially something nice. It sounded odd, yet beautiful at the same time.

Manuela had finally rocked Maria Elisabeth to sleep. Even she was tiring, but that was to be expected at 11:00 p.m.

Manuela hinted to her family that it was time to go to bed. "Tomorrow will bring Christmas morning," she said.

James and Eduardo put away the video games and prepared to go to sleep as well. James Sr. and Jose were left behind in the kitchen. Jose described the needed car repairs. As it turned out, the car needed a new starter. It would take Jose another week before he could earn the money to replace it. Although he was disturbed by the car's recent troubles, he was thankful that his family was safe and warm. That was most important to him.

The wind continued to whistle outside the doors and windows, beckoning to enter. The heat was on, but there was still a slight chill in the house. James Sr. told his son to get more blankets from the basement closet. And that's where he found them! Hidden presents for him from his mom! He was so excited that he ran to his father's bedroom, presents in hand.

"Dad, can I open them? Can I open them now?" he questioned, glowing with vibrant joy. He marveled at how well his father had kept this secret from him, despite his recent and persistent complaining.

"Yes, I suppose you can open them now. I would if I were you," his father said with raised eyebrows and a Cheshire grin.

"You knew they were here all along, Dad! I'm sorry about how I've been behaving lately," James confessed.

His father nodded and gestured for him to open the presents. James opened his gifts frantically, but only to his disappointment.

"Well…what did you get?" his father inquired as he peeked over James's shoulder.

James checked the boxes thoroughly once again to make sure he wasn't missing anything. He was not mistaken. He received a total of three gifts: a coat, a pair of sneakers, and a new book entitled, *The Christmas Gift,* by Louis Raphael

"What's the matter? Don't you like them?" his father asked.

"Yeah, Dad, they're really nice. The coat has great colors, and my sneakers will match anything. And I can read this book if I get bored on a snowy day like today," he answered simply.

"So why the long face?" his father asked.

"Well, I guess I thought…" James hesitated, not wanting to seem dissatisfied. "I guess I already have a coat *and* black sneakers. Why didn't Mom think to get me something different…special, you know, like something I may have *really* wanted or could use more? I'm not trying to sound ungrateful, Dad, really." he explained.

"James, your mother did get you some special things. She got you what she thought you needed, and from what I see, you could use them."

James looked surprised at his father's comment. First he gave her a compliment. Now he was agreeing with her in her absence? Moreover, how could his dad think they were the right choices? Especially when he already had those things?

"You can use them to teach yourself about *thankfulness* and *giving*. Your mother chose those gifts with careful thought and love from her heart—that's how to give! Now you can learn more about how to be thankful for her thoughtfulness and love. For example, you can learn from the Rodriguez family. Their situation isn't what they expected or wanted, but nevertheless, they are thankful for what they have and what has been given to them tonight.

"Now I know there are some things you really want to have, and I'm sure you'll get some of them when you least expect it. I still have a gift for you, too, but it's kind of a surprise. You'll get it tomorrow when we come back home from taking Jose and his family home. In the meantime, remember how much more meaningful it is to know that someone thought you were special enough to receive not one, but three gifts! And that someone is your mom! How many times has Mom ever been wrong? We all could learn a lot from her. She's full of surprises. Do you get what I'm saying to you, Jimmy?" his father asked.

"Yes, Dad!" James said, smiling. Now that was three—three times his father said something in favor of his mom, and he liked it! "You're right, Dad! Mom really does think a lot about doing her best for people. I understand better now. So…can I tell Mom that you said she's never wrong?" he said teasingly.

"No, no, no. I didn't say that, did I?" he said with a grin. "Why don't you go to bed before you come up with any other bright ideas."

They laughed as James Sr. gave his son a hug. James went to his room with gifts in hands. As he put his new coat and sneakers away, thinking of his mother, he whispered, "Thanks, Mom! You're the best!"

He put his pajamas on and brought *The Christmas Gift* to bed with him. He got cozy underneath his Buffalo Bills NFL blanket (a previous gift from his mom). Remembering how she would read with him before he went to bed, he pretended she was there with him. He cut on his tiny reading light, clipped it onto the book, and began to read.

SILENT NIGHT, HOLY NIGHT

It was very late, and at first James felt very sleepy. But as he began to read his book, he became more and more alert. The weather outside had taken a turn as well. The storm had died down, and it was no longer snowing. The streets were quiet and still. James opened his bedroom window to get a better view of the winter wonderland surrounding him. Snow trapped by the windowpane trickled onto his "café con leche" colored skin. He could feel the snowflakes slowly melt in his hair and on his cheeks like mini marshmallows in hot cocoa.

The air was crisp and cold. He had to breathe in slowly so as not to choke from the chilling air sweeping through his nostrils and down his windpipe. He exhaled with a cough, watching the cloud of smoke his hot breath made as it cut through the atmosphere. He loved everything about winter. And with one last breath, he closed the window so as not to let the heat escape from his cozy room.

His room was partially aglow from the moon's reflection on the fresh, glistening white snow. The room was warm, and his pillows seemed to snuggle up against his body, cradling him in comfort. There was never a better night, it seemed, to fall into a deep, restful sleep! But he couldn't sleep! Much to his own amazement, James was really intrigued by the book his mother gave him. Maybe it was because the story took place during Christmas time, or maybe it was because his mother would have read it in full to him if she were here this night. Or perhaps it simply *was* interesting and had meaning far beyond any fiction book he had been glued to for hours or even days.

James's eyes were fixed to every page as the story took him through a young girl's journey to her grandmother's for Christmas, where she learned about Jesus' birth and her family's celebratory traditions. Hers was a simple but large African American family—like his father's family back in Buffalo.

There were many similarities between the character's family experiences and his own. Reading the book caused him to reminisce of times his family got together for the holidays and other special events. There was lots of fun to have, an abundance of food, and plenty of cousins to play with. As for traditions, well, he couldn't really remember the family calling any particular activity a tradition, but he knew his aunt's five-cheese baked macaroni definitely was a consideration!

James began to wonder what really made a family tradition special. Surely there had to be more meaning and purpose to a holiday tradition than just macaroni and cheese, even if it did have five different cheeses in it! So he increasingly became more determined to finish reading the book to find out. He didn't have school the next day, and for now he wasn't tired. In fact, he was wired up! Having guests over and knowing that the next morning was going to be Christmas Day could undoubtedly make any kid an anxious insomniac.

It was very, very late when James finished the book! He even bookmarked the pages that described one of the traditions he liked the most. He was hopeful that by adopting the Basket of Christmases Past and Present tradition (as he called it) into his own family, he could practically guarantee that he would get to spend every Christmas with both his parents, instead of separately on alternating years!

The tradition called for each family member to have a Christmas basket they would have to bring to the Christmas Eve dinner. Each family member would be assigned to purchase or make a gift for another family member. Each gift would serve a purpose and act as a reminder of the reason for the season. At the Christmas Eve dinner, everyone would gather around to share tales about the gift they received last year and the one they received that evening. They would have to tell who gave them the basket and how their baskets would remind others of the reason for the season. Every year, each family member would bring back their baskets with last year's gift and wait to see what new gift would be added to the basket!

What a clever way to remind everyone about the true meaning of Christmas—love, James thought. Immediately, James remembered his mother's words on the telephone earlier that day. *Don't cry. Don't cry!* he commanded himself, but it was too late. He pulled the covers over his shoulder and face. James sunk deeper down into his bed so as to hide his crying eyes from the moon that peaked through his window. He gently closed his eyes. Teardrops twinkled in the corners as they pooled together and ran down to his ears. He prayed to God with thanksgiving for his parents and the Rodriguez family. He prayed for all the people that were sad and alone on Christmas Eve. His tears were beginning to dry on his face as he thanked Jesus for coming and wished Him a happy birthday. And with a deep, releasing sigh, he fell sound asleep.

Good Morning, Christmas!

James's dad was usually the first to wake up in the morning, but James beat him to it. He cut on J93.3FM to hear Christmas songs played all day long. He had already made pancakes and bacon for everyone. The smell of breakfast awakened James's dad and their guests. The Rodriguez family was dressed and ready to head for home. Despite the generous hospitality of James and his father, they didn't want to intrude on their plans to celebrate Christmas.

"Good morning! Merry Christmas. Merry Christmas!" they all said repeatedly to one another.

James's dad announced that they didn't have to rush off. He gladly offered them breakfast and a ride to wherever they needed to go once they were done eating. The Rodriguez's expressed their gratitude and cheerfully sat down to eat Christmas breakfast with them.

James offered to say grace. He thanked God for keeping them safe throughout the night and asked Him to bless the food they were about to enjoy. He also said a prayer for his mom—that she would safely arrive as soon as possible and that he hoped it would be sooner than later. All agreed with a simultaneous "amen," and they began their Christmas feast.

The families shared each other's Christmas morning traditions and described their favorite holiday foods while having breakfast. For the moment, they weren't concerned about the weather or the drive they'd take through the snow-covered streets. They weren't concerned about the time or presents. It was Christmas! That was all that mattered.

The sun suddenly interrupted them with brilliant beams of light shining onto their faces through the dining room windows. James excused himself from the table and went to take a look outside. He put his warm hand on the window to gauge the outside temperature. It was still very cold out. The wind had stopped whistling overnight, but the snow was still out there, keeping company with the much-anticipated ice. James was glad his father offered to take the stranded family home. This was his first Christmas without his own family and Mom around. As they all continued to enjoy eating their Christmas breakfast together, James wondered to himself if the visiting family was anxious to celebrate Christmas Day with their own family and friends. *But for now, we're all they've got.*

"Breakfast was delicious, James. We thank you both very much!" Mr. Rodriguez said.

Everyone couldn't help but notice James grinning wildly at the table. He was so excited he looked (and even felt) as if he were about to burst!

"James, what's goin' on with you, man? Are you okay? We don't want our guests to think you're crazy or something, right? They haven't even met your mother's side of the family yet, so you were practically in the clear," his father said jokingly, although he was truly curious as to what James had up his sleeves.

Almost immediately, James jumped out of his seat and turned toward the Rodriguez family and said, "I have gifts for you before you go! Please wait here!"

James ran to his room to gather his gifts. His father excused himself from the table and followed closely behind, wondering what in the world his son was talking about.

"James, why did you tell them you have gifts for them? I know you didn't go out shopping, and I know you didn't order anything online with my credit cards, because you do value your life, don't you?" he said sarcastically.

James laughed. His mother and father had a very natural way of being sarcastic even in the most seemingly serious situations and circumstances. He continued to scurry about in his room in a hunting-and-gathering type fashion while his father stood there puzzled and anxiously awaiting an explanation.

"Dad, you were right!" he explained. "I needed to learn about the true meaning of Christmas! It's about love, Dad!" James ran past his father, who was standing in the doorway of his room, with gifts in hand once again. This time, they were for giving instead of receiving.

He presented Manuela with a beautiful hat, scarf, and gloves set. She smiled and gave James a kiss on his cheek, speaking to him in Spanish. He hadn't mastered Spanish; he recognized some of the words but was still building his vocabulary and learning how to conjugate verbs. He turned and looked at her son for clarity through interpretation.

"She says you are a sweet boy and she will cherish your gift always!" Eduardo reported.

James smiled and handed Eduardo a box. James and Eduardo were about the same age and had similar interests, so he was sure this gift would please his guest. It was wrapped in construction paper, since it was all James had in his room. James was half-asleep when he wrapped it earlier that morning, anyway, so he figured it was the gift that counted and thought nothing more of it.

He watched as Eduardo unwrapped it and was eager to see his reaction. When Eduardo opened his gift he was indeed surprised and incredibly happy! Inside the box was a new coat and a new pair of sneakers inside. He tried them on and they fit perfectly!

James's father watched as his son handed out presents, thinking they looked awfully familiar. He couldn't believe what James was doing, and even more surprising was he didn't mind at all.

"Thanks, man! Wow, I really could use these things on a day like today! Were these yours?" he asked James.

"No," he replied. "My mom sent them for someone that needed them, and I figured that someone was you!"

James handed Manuela another gift. This one was for the baby. "What is the baby's name, again?" he asked Mrs. Rodriguez.

"Maria Elisabeth," she said softly.

He pulled out a shiny silver picture frame ornament, which he had recently purchased at the mall. James originally bought it for his mom to hang on her Christmas tree, but figured he would still have time to get her another one. The engraved message fittingly read, "Christmas 2014." James then pulled out a fine-point black permanent marker and wrote, "1st," in front of the engraved words. On the back of the ornament he wrote, "Maria Elisabeth," as Eduardo spelled it out loud.

Then James got his father's camera and hurried everyone into a family portrait pose. He set the camera's timer and strategically placed it on the fireplace mantle. He quickly scrambled to find a place in their huddle before the camera could take their picture. Once in position, they all counted to three, and the flash captured their moment of Christmas joy. James gave the camera to his father so he could print the photo from his computer. Once printed, they placed the picture in the frame for Maria Elisabeth.

"Now she will always want to hear the story of her first Christmas, and we will always remember each other," James announced.

Everyone smiled and admired his thoughtfulness. Even his father was impressed and touched by the seemingly overnight transformation of his son's outlook on Christmas. He even looked all around and under the tables to make sure his real son wasn't tied up somewhere by the imposter that was running around giving away selfless gifts.

"Thank you. Thank you so much for your gifts to my family. May God bless you for all your love," Mr. Rodriguez said with compassion in his voice.

"Oh, wait! One more gift! I have a gift for you too, Mr. Rodriguez!" James said.

In an instant, James flew up the stairs and swept through his room, searching for a reminder of Mr. Rodriguez's gift. How could he not remember what he had planned to give Mr. Rodriguez? This moment was becoming increasingly awkward for him, and even though there wasn't any pressure to give, he began to sweat. For the first time he could truly appreciate why his mother and father would never let him stay up too late. It obviously affects your thinking. His father began to call for him, and he could hear them all laughing and singing Christmas songs, but he wasn't ready.

He just needed a few seconds to think and it would come back to him.

James sat down at his desk and looked around the room one last time, hoping to remember. His heart was beating loudly at an accelerated rate. He covered his ears and closed his eyes in an attempt to quiet himself and drown out all other distractions. He took three deep breaths, and at his last exhale he could almost hear his heart pounding slower and slower. It reminded him of a giant clock ticking loudly and scolding him as if he were running out of time. Time! What time was it, anyway? James looked at his clock and saw it. He remembered now! Beside his alarm clock was the secret box where he kept his prized possessions: card collections, cologne sample bottles, and his money clip! He hastily snatched the clip and it's contents from the box. Then he reached for his piggy bank and made a withdrawal. Dashing out of his room, he also reached for the small gift he wrapped earlier that morning for his dad.

There was lots of clanking and crashing noises coming from James's room down the corridor. Suddenly, James came flying back into the living room where everyone was still gathered together. Inside a large Ziploc bag, James had collected all the bills and coins he had been saving and presented them to Mr. Rodriguez.

"This is a gift toward helping fix your car. I was saving it for a video game I wanted, but I don't need that as much as you and your family need the car," James confessed.

Mr. Rodriguez gestured that he could not accept the money, but before he could say much of anything, James pleaded, "Please take this gift. Families help each other all the time. Today we are your family, and I want you to have my gift, because it is all I have to give you. Please take it."

Mr. Rodriguez was speechless. James Sr. nodded in approval and with great pride in his son's maturity. He put his arm around James and hugged him. Manuela was so moved by his generosity that she began to cry silent tears of joy. Eduardo looked to his father and asked if he wanted him to translate for him. Jose nodded and spoke in Spanish as he looked at James and his father.

"My father says he is very grateful to your family. He says your son has a very generous heart and will grow to be a man God will use greatly, but he cannot accept the hard-earned money of a child."

James's father responded quickly, "I can understand your thinking. James is encouraged to spend his money wisely and unselfishly. Please accept his gift and mine as a blessing from our family to yours." James's father took out a hundred dollar bill from his wallet and gave it to Jose along with the Ziploc bag of money. "Please take it and be blessed by it," he continued.

The whole family looked on as Eduardo interpreted for his parents and waited for his dad's response. Jose nodded in acceptance of the monetary gifts and shook their hands, thanking them on behalf of his family. At that very moment

James could feel the love, joy, and gratitude that filled the cozy sunlit room. Suddenly, Christmas seemed different for James. It was an experience like no other Christmas he had ever celebrated before. And that was okay.

"Wait," Eduardo interrupted. "We have nothing to give you in return!"

James could see more clearly now what Christmas was all about! He fully understood what his dad meant the night before. He didn't want Jose to feel bad or ashamed because his family had nothing to give them in return. That wasn't what it was about. In an instant, James was reminded of the Christmas song his mother loved the most (even though she loved hundreds) that was helpful at this very moment.

"Have you ever heard a Christmas song about an orphan girl named Maria called *The Gift*?" James asked Mr. Rodriguez.

He nodded with uncertainty and confusion. He didn't know what that had to do with anything. Everyone else in the room seemed to be equally confused.

"Well, this song tells the story of a girl named Maria who had nothing to give to baby Jesus on Christmas Eve. Everyone else would have brought what they thought were special gifts, but all she had was a caged bird. That bird sang the most beautiful song. It was like an offering fit for a king. Like Maria, you have given us your gift already. You accepted our invitation to come here and made this Christmas so much fun for me, more fun than I thought it could be. You gave us your gift of friendship," James explained.

"Yes, you have!" said James's dad. "You've taught us so much about the true spirit of Christmas. We've all learned more about giving, gratitude, compassion, and God's love all in one night! I agree with James that you've made this a very special Christmas for us."

Eduardo interpreted to his family what James and his father had said. They smiled and nodded in agreement.

"Besides," James said, "We needed your help to eat all of that pizza!"

Everyone laughed for what seemed like forever. It was now 10:30 a.m. It was time to prepare for their journey in the snow to take the Rodriguez family to their home.

THE GREATEST CHRISTMAS GIFT

The snow was bright white and seemed even brighter as the sunlight reflected off it. The air was clean, cold, and brisk, but not blustery. It was just right. The birds were singing happily as if they were a well-rehearsed choir performing for a grand celebration. It was otherwise a quiet and serene morning—beautiful, to be exact!

James took a deep breath, filling his lungs with Christmas morning, and he slowly exhaled Christmas peace. He wondered what this Christmas morning was like for his mother. *I have to call Mom as soon as we get back.*

Once everyone was safe and secure in the car, James and his father began to escort the Rodriguez family to their home. It was a forty-five-minute drive, most of which they spent not talking. James, of course, had to turn the radio to 104.7 FM so they could hear endless Christmas songs during the ride. Everyone was relaxed. Some fell asleep, but not James. He enjoyed the company of the Rodriguez family, but was feeling the cold reality of not having his mom around for Christmas. He thought about how much they would have loved to meet her. He was beginning to miss her all over again. He couldn't wait to tell her all that had happened. What would she think about what he did with her gifts? He hoped she would understand, but for now, he planned to just enjoy the ride.

Despite the chaos that usually occurs in Georgia whenever there is snowfall, James's father brought them to their destination safely. Mrs. Rodriguez gave James the tightest hug he'd had since his mother was in Georgia. She pinched his cheek and gave him a kiss as well. James blushed and hugged her back. The boys and men shook hands and exchanged numbers. Their good-byes were brief yet heartfelt. Waving farewell to their friends, James and his father crunched through the thick snow toward the car. Once inside, they buckled their seatbelts and repositioned their seats as they prepared for the wintry travel back toward home.

Now it was almost noon, and James was beginning to feel incredibly sleepy. He welcomed the serene ride home. James turned up the radio to hear another one of his favorite Christmas carols. Driving down the wintry roads, he caught glimpses of children making angels in the snow and having snowball wars. Occasionally, their car would fall victim to random attacks by snowball warriors and their stray snowballs while they were forced to halt at stop signs and crosswalks. Now he couldn't wait to have his own snowball fight with his dad. Suddenly, he wasn't sleepy anymore. He felt refreshed and invigorated.

Almost home, he thought. There weren't very many cars driving on the roads, but it was still a slow trip back. It wasn't snowing, but it was increasingly difficult to see for a distance of about two to four cars ahead. Nevertheless, James could tell they were closer to home. As they drove a few more blocks, he noticed his father made a turn on a street to which he was unfamiliar. He didn't ask why. He considered his father chose an alternate, safer route. Thinking nothing more of it, he took this opportunity to admire all the beautifully decorated homes along the way.

Other than the Christmas music and brief commentary heard during the radio commercials, the ride was otherwise void of conversation. But that suddenly came to an end. His father's cell phone rang, and he pulled over to answer it. James thought this was odd since his father would usually ignore his gentle reprimands about texting and talking while driving. He watched his father pace in front and around the car as he talked. He didn't know who his dad was talking to, but it must have been important, because he was whispering and covering the phone while he talked, even though there was no one outside to hear him.

After a few minutes, he checked the time and wondered what his mom was doing. She hadn't called, and neither had he. He never really stopped to think how she might be feeling without him there this Christmas. He hoped she wasn't feeling sad or lonely. He closed his eyes and said a prayer for her. Just as he was done, his father hurried back inside the car, startling him. Then, out of the blue, his father smiled at him and rubbed his head really hard.

"Dad! Cut it out!" James shouted, jokingly protesting his father's loving gesture.

"Son, I've been thinking about last night and this morning, and I've got to tell you I'm very proud of you!"

James grinned from ear to ear with great joy from hearing his father's praise.

"What encouraged you to give away your things *and* your money? I almost wondered if you were really my son there for a minute!" his father said with a wide grin.

"Well, I kept remembering all the things you and Mom said yesterday. After reading the book Mom gave me, I figured that I should be thoughtful and give them something they needed. So I tried to think about what I could give, and I didn't want to give them any of my old stuff, so I gave away the new coat and sneakers Mom sent me. The money was the only thing I had that I thought Mr. Rodriguez could use, and the hat, gloves, and scarf set was for Mom, but I gave it to Mrs. Rodriguez instead. Which reminds me, Dad, I have a gift for you too!" James pulled the small wrapped gift from out of his pocket. He handed the festive gift box to his father, saying, "Merry Christmas,

Dad." His father was surprised that James had something for him. He always told James he didn't have to give him a gift for Christmas because all he wanted was world peace, but James's mom taught him to always honor and celebrate his father. So inside the box was a small acrylic globe on a stand that he and his mother picked out at the mall a month before. It read: "World Peace: Christmas 2014." His father smiled when he saw it and gave James a long, hard hug. "Thank you, son. I guess now I get to see the world at peace," his father said. James chuckled and agreed.

James now realized that he didn't have a gift for his mother, nor did he have any money left to buy her another one. "Do you think Mom will understand when I tell her I don't have a gift for her?" he asked.

"Your mother? She could never be mad at you for that. As a matter of fact, not only do I think she would understand, I know she'd be very proud of you! But you know what? You don't have to believe me. Why don't you tell her and find out for yourself right now?"

James's father parked the car in front of a snow-covered blue house in a neighborhood close to his own. James patiently waited for his father to find his cell phone and hand it over so that he could call his mother. Instead, he got out of the car and motioned for James to do the same. James was puzzled, but he obeyed. He got out of the car and followed behind his dad, who was walking up the driveway of the big, blue, snow-covered house.

In the driveway was a huge U-Haul truck. It hardly had any snow on it. James figured someone must have just driven it here very early this morning, when the storm ceased. But who? His father didn't mention a stop along the way.

Who were they going to see in this house, anyway? he thought. *And who would be moving or driving a huge U-Haul truck on Christmas day? Why can't I just stay in the car and call Mom?*

James was beginning to hope this was all a cruel joke as he drudged up the driveway. Surely they weren't going to spend the day moving furniture for one of his dad's friends...or were they? He ran to catch up to his father.

"Dad! Dad! I thought you wanted me to call Mom to ask her myself?" he asked impatiently.

They were standing at the front door. His father wiped his feet on the welcome rug and motioned for James to do the same. Then he rang the doorbell three times. James could not understand why his father was ignoring him.

"I do want you to talk to your mother, James," his father said. "That's why we're here!"

Now James was really confused! His father still hadn't handed him the cell phone, and he couldn't help but wonder why they would need to go to someone else's home to call his mom. Was his cell phone dead? Did his car charger not work? These and other thoughts raced through his mind, but he couldn't figure it out. His father peaked in the windows alongside the door as if to check that someone was indeed at home and might come to the door. James was beginning to feel angry and just had to ask his father once more.

"Dad, I don't understand. Can I *please* speak to Mom?"

His father rocked back and forth and smiled at James as if he didn't know his son had said a thing to him. Christmas music was playing from inside the house and seemed to be seeping through the door. They both could hear it, but it wasn't comforting James one bit. He glared at his father, awaiting a response or even an explanation as to why they were standing out in the cold in front of some stranger's door, a stranger who obviously wasn't home because he wasn't answering. James asked again, "Dad, can I please speak to Mom now?"

The door began to unlock. Grinning wildly, his father replied, "Sure, son...go ahead."

The door opened slowly, and much to his disbelief and amazement his mother was standing in the doorway. "Hi, baby boy!" she said with arms opened wide to receive him.

"Mom! It's you! You're here! You're here with us for Christmas!" James lunged at his mom and tackled her with a strong, yet loving embrace.

"Surprise!" his mom exclaimed. "Now you'll have two homes in the same city and state. Not too many children I know have two bedrooms they can keep a mess!"

The reunited family giggled at her remark. Then James slowly released her and stepped back to look at her once more as if to make sure she were real lest she vanish before his very eyes. His face was aglow with pure joy and excitement.

He turned toward his father and gave him an intense finger scolding, then hugged him tightly, saying, "Thanks, Dad! This was a great surprise. I love you, Dad!" He ran back toward his mother and held her once again, saying, "I love you, too, Mom! Now we'll always be together for Christmas!"

James knew his mother moving here did not mean that his parents weren't getting a divorce, but he knew it was a step in the right direction. At that very moment he realized that even if they did divorce, they still loved him, and if they could communicate as well as they did to keep this secret from him, they might be able to at least be friends. Whatever their relationship would become, he knew they'd always be family and that hope still had a powerful place in his life.

His tearful embrace with his mother remained tight and long. They all came into the warm, cozy house and his father closed the door behind them.

As they walked toward the living room, James couldn't help but notice the moving boxes scattered all over the house, except for the living room. It was obvious that the only ones opened were the ones that stored all of Mom's Christmas stuff. Family photos, Christmas stockings, and all of James's handmade holiday creations were strategically displayed on the fireplace mantle. Shining brightly and lighting up the room was the Christmas tree, off to the left of the fireplace. It was adorned with ornaments Mom collected over the years. Each ornament represented a family member, special event or memento from a past Christmas. James thought it was the most beautiful Christmas tree he had ever seen. There weren't any presents under it—just a small nativity scene passed down to him from his paternal grandmother, Grandma Gwen. It was something he always treasured. It was perfect!

James didn't even notice that there weren't any presents. As they sat on the couch in front of the fireplace, they drank hot chocolate and ate cinnamon rolls. He was so very happy! He had so much to tell his mother and wanted to ask his parents how they planned this secret surprise, but he couldn't just yet.

As James gave his mother another hug, his father joined in, making it a group hug. He held on to his parents, cherishing the moment, never wanting to let them go. He remained there, smothered in his parents' embrace.

His muffled voice spoke words from deep within his heart, and the sentiment expressed rang loud and clear. "Having you both here, together with me, is the greatest Christmas gift of all!"

There's no greater gift than love.